The Dog I Share

JANICE MARRIOTT

illustrated by Phillip Small

Learning Media

It happened like this ....

I looked out of our window on the fifth floor. Way down below, a man and a dog were walking up the path to the ground-floor apartment. The dog was yellow, with loopy ears and a swinging tail.

The dog looked up and saw me. I waved – not my tail, just my arm.

"Mom, I'm going to play with the new people on the ground floor."

I ran out the door and into the elevator. That dog was wanting to play with me. I just knew it.

Floor 5 – we were going to play tug of war with an old towel.

Floor 2 – we were going to run around the parking lot, doing very fast turns.

I knocked on the door to the ground-floor apartment. I was panting and smiling at the same time. I knew a dog would like that.

A thin man opened the door. I couldn't see his eyes because he was wearing dark glasses. Somehow, I could tell he was staring at me. The dog was beside him.

I panted and smiled. I almost barked. "I live on the fifth floor," I told him. He wasn't very friendly. He told me I couldn't play with his dog. His dog wasn't for playing with.

"Go home!" he said.

"We'll see about that," I thought, as I waited for the elevator. I watched the little lights go 5, 4, 3, 2, 1. Ping! The doors opened.

"See ya later," I said as I stepped inside. I wasn't going to be put off by a thin guy wearing sunglasses in a dark room.

Chapter 2

The next day, my friend Gracie on the seventh floor told me that the new guy was blind.

"So what?" I said.

"I nearly went smack into him," said Gracie. "He didn't get out of the way of my chair when Hughie was pushing me. That's how I found out."

I went to see the blind guy, but he still didn't look pleased to see me.

"It's me again. Hey, man," I said. "I know that dog of yours is a guide dog. I know she leads you around. She works hard. I thought she might like a friend to throw her a ball sometimes."

The man said, "Come in." I couldn't tell he was blind. He knew where the doors were, the door handles, the cups and glasses, even the faucet.

While we were drinking orange juice, I bent down and stroked the dog. Her skin moved loosely on her back. Her brown nose was lying on two big round paws. Her tail rose and thumped down on the floor.

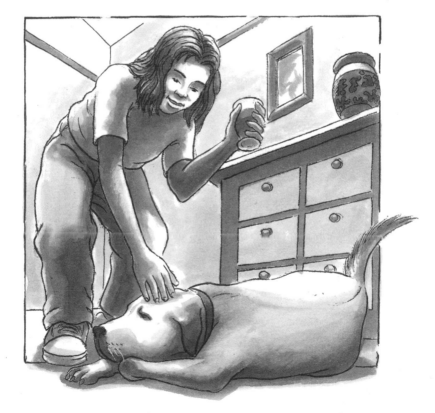

"Don't touch the dog," he said.

"Can I walk her sometimes?" I asked.

"No," he said. "I can't let her out of my sight. Ha, ha!"

"Very funny," I said. I was put off by the real bitterness in his voice. "OK. I'm leaving," I said. I could tell it was time to go. I looked at the dog. I grinned at her. She lifted her head and grinned at me.

When she grinned, her mouth opened, and her tongue lay gently along the tops of her teeth. She had big creases in her face, by her eyes and at the corners of her mouth. It made me feel good just to look at her. I wanted to take her with me.

Chapter 3

The next day, Gracie was hanging out at my place. We looked out of the window and saw the blind guy walk down his path. He walked out his little gate and off down the road.

That beautiful yellow dog went too, walking slowly, her tail swinging. She was wearing a harness, and the man held onto a handle that came out of the harness. I decided to follow them.

"Mom, we're just off to the park," I shouted. "Come on, Gracie. Get in your chair."

Down. 5, 4, 3, 2, 1. Ping!

I pushed Grace out of the building, and there they were at the corner, waiting for the lights to change.

The dog was standing beside the man.

I wondered how the dog would know when the lights were green.

I'd read somewhere that dogs are color-blind.

I kept my distance. When the lights changed, the man said something to the dog, and they started off across the road. The dog walked just in front of the man.

I knew she was enjoying her walk because her back wiggled and her tail waggled.

The man passed the newsstand and stopped at the fruit shop.

He went in, and so did the yellow dog!

Into the shop!

I parked Gracie in her chair on the sidewalk and hurried after them.

The man bought two bananas and some oranges. As he turned to leave the shop, the woman behind the counter said, "Hello, Becky." I had to say, "Hello, Mrs. Carrasco."

The man said, "I thought she was following us." Then he turned around. "It's you, girl, isn't it, from the apartment building?" That guy was so unfriendly. "Why don't you leave us alone?" he yelled. His voice was weird. He sounded kind of scared.

"Will do!" I yelled back. The guy was crazy. Why would he be scared of me? I'm the smallest kid in my grade. As I left the shop, I smiled – for the dog.

Chapter 4

I waited with Gracie around the corner till they'd gone past.

I waited to see them cross the road again.

I guess I needed to know the dog had got across safely.

Then I bought a comic book at the newsstand and we went home.

When we got to our building, I saw the man on his porch.

He was kneeling down, patting the concrete step.

The yellow dog was standing beside him, very patient.

I knew what had happened.

"He can wait while I take Gracie up," I thought.

She thought I was ignoring him, and she let me have it real good when we were in the elevator.

"Me, be kind to the disabled?" I said, and we both laughed.

"Bye, Gracie!" I left her with her mom and went back down.

7, 6, 5, 4, 3, 2, 1. Ping!

I knew Gracie would watch the buttons light up to make sure I didn't stop at the fifth floor.

He was still there, patting the step.

I walked down his path. "It's me, Beck[...]
said. I patted the dog and gently pulled her long[...]
silky ears. While I did this, I was looking around.

The key was glinting in the sunlight. It wasn't
on the step. It had fallen off into the flower bed.

"Here you are," I said. "Your key."

"Thank you, Becky."

"No big deal. Anyone could have seen it."

"Not me," he said.

Then he smiled.

He got up, holding onto the key. He put it into
the keyhole, no trouble at all.

Chapter 5

He was a different person. He chatted while he took off the dog's harness and made a coffee. He said it was hard moving to a new area. Sorry he'd been grumpy.

"I haven't been blind long. I'm not very good at it yet."

"How did you ...?"

"Someone beat me up real bad."

What could I say? There was total silence.

"Shall I open these cookies?" I was desperate.

"What sort are they?"

"Chocolate chip."

"Sure thing."

He told me not to feed the dog. "Sascha is very highly trained. You could mess that up if you offered her cookies all the time."

"I can work *that* out," I said. I stroked her neck. She turned her head and licked my hand and looked at me.

"I couldn't do anything without her," he said. "That's why I have to be careful who I trust her with."

"You can trust me," I said. "And Gracie. That's my friend in the wheelchair you crashed into."

"I remember."

Sascha slid down onto the floor, rolled over, and grinned at me.

"She looks so cute," I said. Then I wished I hadn't said it. I felt awkward. We ate the cookies.

"She does need extra walks," he said. "But perhaps it's better if you just come visiting until we all get to know each other."

"Sure thing."

I told him where I lived and recorded my phone number onto his tape recorder ... in case he needed any high-speed deliveries done – or anything at all. Even opening packets of cookies. I patted Sascha again and said goodbye.

And slowly, over a whole year, that's how I got to be the "chief minder" of a guide dog.